# JAKE IS LATE

**Story by Charles LaBelle**
**Illustration by Chris Hayes**

*The Storyteller*

1995 Charles J. LaBelle

Original Publication   1995 *The Storyteller*
117-3691 Albion Rd.
Gloucester, Ont. KIT 1P2
613-733 -0410

**Canadian Cataloguing in Publication Data**

**LaBelle, Charles, J. 1939-**
      **Jake Is Late**
**1st ed.**
**ISBN 1-896710-00-X**

      **1.Picture books for children.  I. Hayes, Chris
II. Title.**

**PS8573.A157J34 1995        jC813'.54        C95-900986-8
PR9199.3.L22J34 1995**

Printed and bound in Canada by
Tyrell Press Ltd.
2714 Fenton Rd.
Gloucester, Ont.
(613) 822-0740

To Jake and Jack
and children who are late.

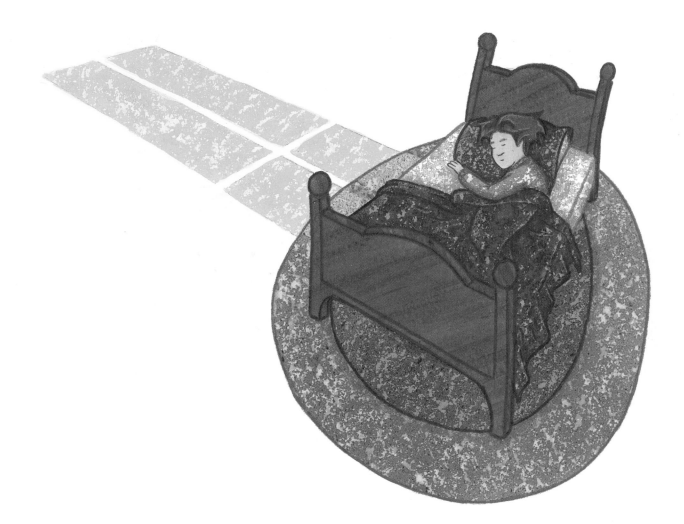

Jake's mother called up the stairs.

"Jake, Jake, you will be late!"

Jake rolled over in bed and answered, **"Piff piff, boom boom! Don't worry Mom, I'll be there soon."**

He looked up and counted the paper spit balls that were stuck to his ceiling.

"One, two, three, four, five, six, seven, eight, nine, ten."

Jake went into the bathroom and sat on the toilet.

He counted the tiles on the shower wall.

"One, two, three, four...."

Mom called up the stairs.

"Jake, Jake, you will be late."

Jake answered, **"Piff piff, boom boom! Don't worry Mom, I'll be there soon."**

Jake started to brush his teeth. Then he stopped and began to count them.

"One, two, three, four, five, six, seven, eight, nine, ten."

Mom called, "Jake, Jake, you will be late."

Jake answered, **"Piff piff, boom boom! Don't worry Mom, I'll be there soon."**

Jake counted the drops of water that dripped from the tap.

He counted the shower curtain hooks and finally finished in the bathroom.

Jake went to his room and counted as he got dressed.

"One for the socks, two for the shoes, three for the gloves, four for the underwear, five for the scarf, six for the shirt, seven for the sweater, eight for the hat, nine for the coat and ten for....

What is ten for?"

Jake scratched his head and thought, "I can't remember."

Jake turned left out of his room, then he turned right and counted down the stairs.

One, two, three, four, five, six, seven, eight, nine, ten.

Mom went to the bottom of the stairs. Mom looked Jake right in the eye.

"Jake, Jake, you will be late," she said.

Jake answered, **"Piff piff, boom boom! Don't worry Mom, I'll be there soon."**

Jake ate his breakfast and counted the seeds in his orange juice.

He counted the Cherryos in his bowl.

He counted the berries in his yogurt.

He counted the buttons on the stove. He counted the tiles on the floor and he counted the knobs on the cupboards.

He was just beginning to count the pots and pans in the pot rack when Mom said, "Jake, Jake, you will be late."

Jake answered, "**Piff piff, boom boom! Don't worry Mom, I'll be there soon**."

"Get your books and wait outside for the school bus," Mom said.

Jake went up the stairs, two at a time, counting as he climbed.

"Two, four, six, eight, ten." Then he turned to the right, then he turned to the left and then he was in his room.

Jake couldn't find his books.

He knew the Hiding Monster hid them while he was sleeping.

Jake sat on the bed and thought about what the Hiding Monster might look like.

Did the Hiding Monster have long sharp teeth? Did the Hiding Monster have red eyes and a big nose?

Jake heard a noise. Jake was scared. Jake was afraid to look under the bed for his books.

Mom called, "Jake, Jake, you will be late."

Jake answered softly, "Piff piff, boom boom. Don't worry Mom, I'll be there soon."

He looked under the bed and saw a dark shape at the back.

Jake jumped back and yelled, **"Mom there's a monster under my bed!"**

Mom came running up the stairs, two at a time, with a broom in her hand.

"Two, four, six, eight, ten!" she counted.

Mom turned to the right, then turned to the left and was in Jake's room.

Mom shouted, "Don't worry Jake, I'll get him with my broom."

Mom shoved the broom under the bed and smashed it from side to side.

Jake looked under the bed and said, **"Piff piff, boom boom! The monster must have left the room."**

Mom looked under the bed.

"Look Jake! We must have scared the Hiding Monster right out of his clothes."

Mom reached under the bed and pulled out:

two different coloured socks,

three pair of underwear,

one pair of pyjamas,

three shirts, and

one pair of pants.

"That adds up to ten," said Jake.

"You are so clever," said Mom.

"Jake, Jake, you will be late. Where are your books?"

"The Hiding Monster ate them," said Jake laughing.

"Piff piff, boom boom! Don't worry Mom, I'll find them soon. Oh! I remember now. I put them by the door last night, so I wouldn't forget where they were."

"Jake, Jake, you will be late," said Mom.

"Piff piff, boom boom! Don't worry Mom, I'll be there soon," said Jake.

Jake and his mom counted backward down the stairs. "Ten, nine, eight, seven, six, five, four, three, two, one."

Just then they heard the school bus blowing its horn.

"Jake, Jake, you **ARE** late!" said Mom.

Jake said "Piff piff...."

## Mom screamed!

**"Oh no!**

 **Oh no!**

Jake you forgot to put your pants on.

There goes the bus. Now I'll have to drive you to school."

"Sorry Mom", said Jake and he went to put his pants on.

Mom ran to the car and waited for Jake.

Jake got in the car, but he didn't count anything.

As Mom drove she could see that Jake was very sad and very sorry.

Mom stopped the car in the park beside their favourite duck pond.

Mom said, "Jake, Jake, sometimes it's ok to be late."

Mom took a bag of stale bread from the back seat and said, "Let's go feed the ducks."

Just then, Mom's car phone rang.

It was Mom's Boss.

The boss said, "Kate, Kate, you are late."

Kate said, **"Piff piff, boom boom! Don't worry Boss, I'll be in by noon."**

# Other Jake adventures by Charles LaBelle to follow.

| | | | |
|---|---|---|---|
| Jake Is Cold | Jake Is Lost | Jake Is Hot | Jake Is Hungry |
| Jake Is Sick | Jake Is Sad | Jake is Bad | Jake Is Funny |
| Jake Is Full | Jake Is Scared | Jake Is Stinky | Jake Is Greasy |
| Jake Is Happy | Jake Is Scary | Jake Is Kissed | Jake Is Missed |

Tape Recordings of the stories, personal story telling by the author and prints of all art work are available from *The Storyteller*, 117-3691 Albion Rd. Gloucester, Ont. KIT 1P2, phone 613 733-0410.